STONE ARCH BOOKS
a capstone imprint

Jim Nasium
is published by Stone Arch Books,
a Capstone Imprint
1710 Roe Crest Drive
North Mankato, Minnesota 56003
www.capstoneyoungreaders.com

Cataloging-in-Publication Data is available on
the Library of Congress website.
ISBN: 978-1-4965-0521-7 (reinforced library hardcover)
ISBN: 978-1-4965-0526-2 (paperback)
ISBN: 978-1-4965-2330-3 (eBook)

Summary: Despite his name, Jim Nasium is no all-star athlete.
But he's determined to find the right sport for him in this hilarious
and wacky chapter book adventure! This time he's trying his
uncoordinated hand at basketball. Will Jim be a
hoops hero or a basket case?

Printed in the United States of America in Stevens Point, Wisconsin.
052015   008824WZF15

JIM NASIUM

Is a Basket Case

WRITTEN BY
MARTY McKNIGHT

ART BY
CHRIS JONES

CONTENTS

CHAPTER ONE

THE SIXTEENTH MAN

BREEEEEP! A whistle blared across the gymnasium.

"TIME-OUT!" Coach Pittman shouted from the sideline.

The team hustled off the basketball court and took their places on the bench. I was already there, of course. Someone had to keep the bench warm and toasty for the other players.

Coach placed his hands on his hips, hung his head, and paced back and forth in front of the team. He took a deep breath and exhaled slowly. "We're still in this game, boys," he said, pointing up at the scoreboard.

It read, "HOME 47, VISITORS 46."

Our team was down by one point with eight seconds remaining.

"You've all played a solid game," he told the five starting players, who were panting and wiping sweat from their brows. "But I'm going to mix things up a bit."

Coach Pittman looked down the bench at his lineup of subs.

Did you know that in basketball they have a special name for an important substitute player? You know, the player who comes off the bench, scores oodles of points, and lifts his team to victory. They call that player the sixth man. Well, that's not me.

I glanced down the bench at Coach Pittman's choices: Brad Barker, Ricky Howard, Justin Springfield, Dudley Schumaker, and my best friend, Milo Cabrera. And on, and on, and on.

Sixth man, I thought. *More like the SIXTEENTH man!*

I stared down at my clean, dry uniform and never-touched-the-court high-tops. *Why'd I even bother suiting up?* I wondered.

But then, a tick of the time-out clock later, I heard Coach shout my name — or at least, I thought he'd said my name.

I looked up and — yep! — Coach Pittman was pointing right in my direction.

"Me?" I asked, looking around at the other players.

"You're the only Jim Nasium I know," he said.

***

Yeah, you heard him right. The name's Jim Nasium — don't wear it out!

With a name like mine I should be a sports sensation. You know, a real gym class hero!

The problem is . . . I lack some serious game.

You've heard that old saying "born with two left feet." Well, I was born with two left feet AND two left arms! That's a real problem in basketball — or any sport, for that matter. And I'd know. At this point, I've tried just about every sport on the planet.

The result? Well, let's just say I've warmed some very nice benches in my day.

But this year is going to be different.

This year, I won't be a basket case. I'll be a hoops hero!

CHAPTER TWO

AIR(BALL) JIM

BZZZZZZZRRRRRRRT!!

The buzzer sounded, and the players from both teams hustled back onto the court. (Or, in my case, shuffled very, very slowly.)

One of my teammates stood on the sidelines near midcourt. An official in a black-and-white striped uniform handed him the basketball and blew his whistle.

BREEEEEP!

My other teammates desperately tried to escape their defenders and get open for the inbound pass. They zigged and zagged, squeaking back and forth across the court on their well-worn high-tops.

I stayed put, cuddling up to my defender like a long-lost friend . . . until he gave me a stiff elbow to the ribs. "OOF!"

To be honest, I much preferred the chance of bruised ribs than any chance of getting the ball right then. For the next eight seconds, I would be totally and utterly invisible.

I would be a shadow. A ghost. For the next eight seconds, I'd avoid one thing at all costs —

"The ball?" I muttered.

Somehow, the inbound pass had tipped off the fingers of not one, not two, but three other players and landed in my sweaty, shaky hands.

And just like that the scoreboard clock started ticking:

8 seconds . . .

7 seconds . . .

6 seconds . . .

I stared at the strange orange orb in my hands.

The ball looked like some far-off alien world, and I felt like its first lone explorer. I was completely alone. Just me and that little orange planet. Like Neil Armstrong taking his first step onto the moon. But this wasn't going to be one small step.

This was going to be one BIG disaster!

5 seconds . . .

4 seconds . . .

"Shoot it, Jim!" I heard a familiar voice call from the sidelines.

I glanced over at the bench and spotted Milo and the other subs pointing toward the basket.

3 seconds . . .

2 seconds . . .

I've gotta make this shot, I thought.

Not just for me. I had to make it for Milo, Brad Barker, Ricky Howard, Justin Springfield, Dudley Schumaker, and all the other benchwarmers, sixth men, or SIXTEENTH men out there.

"This one's for you!" I exclaimed.

With one second left on the clock, I extended my arms, flicked my wrist, and the planet-like ball started orbiting toward the basket.

ZRRRRRRRRRT! The final buzzer sounded with the ball in midair.

The shot had perfect backspin, perfect arc, perfect height . . . but far-from-perfect distance.

The ball landed five feet in front of the hoop with a meteoric **THUD!** It bounced two more times and then came to a silent stop on the court.

"AIR BALL!" my archenemy, Bobby Studwell, called out.

"HAHAHA! Good one, Bobby," said his annoying sidekick, Tommy Strong.

Milo stepped onto the court. "I won't argue with you, Bobby," he said, interrupting. "You are the expert on air, after all — HOT air, that is."

Everyone laughed.

"Besides," Milo added, "what's the big deal? It's only practice."

Bobby scoffed. "What are we practicing for . . . losing?"

Tommy snickered again.

BREEEEEEEEEEEEEEEEEEEEEP!

Coach blew his whistle.

"All right, all right. That's enough, gentlemen," he said. "Our first game against the Janesville Jackrabbits is in less than a week, and we have a lot more practicing to do."

Milo raised his hand.

"Yes, Cabrera?" Coach Pittman asked reluctantly.

"Just wondering, Coach," Milo began, "are you suggesting that we HOP to it?"

Milo placed two fingers near his head like jackrabbit ears and began hopping around the court.

"HAHAHA!" Everyone laughed again — everyone, except Coach.

BREEEEEP! Came another whistle.

"Very funny, Cabrera," the coach said, quieting the team. "But the Jackrabbits are no joke. They won the junior league championship last year, and they're predicted to repeat. I need *everyone* at the top of their game if we're going to pull off the upset."

I could've sworn that when Coach Pittman said "everyone," he was looking directly at me.

"Besides," Coach continued, "my dear grandmother will be there, and I'd like you boys to show her a good game."

"Grandmother?!" Milo exclaimed, saying what everyone else was thinking. "*You* have a grandma?"

"Of course I have a grandmother, Cabrera," replied the coach. "*Everyone* has a grandmother."

"I know, Coach, but you're so —" Milo stopped. "I mean, she must be, like, a hundred years old!"

"Tell you what," said the coach, "let's start running laps, and we'll stop when we reach her age."

BREEEEEP! Coach Pittman blew his whistle, and the team groaned.

"Nice going, Cabrera," said Bobby, starting to run.

"What?" said Milo. "Maybe she's younger than we think."

I hoped Milo was right.

CHAPTER THREE

PRACTICE MAKES PAINFUL

He was wrong.

Milo, myself, and the rest of the
Bennett City Buffaloes ran one
hundred and four laps. Well, I actually
ran like the first ten laps, jogged the
next thirty, walked the next fifty,
crawled the next ten and, honestly, I
don't remember the last four.

After practice finally ended, I walked home. (Okay, I actually *limped* home!) I was tired, sore, and hungry, but I had work to do. I may have been born with two left feet AND two left arms, but I couldn't use that as an excuse anymore. After all, a baby bird wasn't born knowing how to fly.

I know that sounded pretty cheesy, but maybe that old saying was true . . . maybe practice really did make perfect. It was worth a shot, right?

Or in my case, many, MANY shots!

I shot another free throw toward the hoop in my driveway.

CLANK!

The basketball bounced off the rim and rolled into the front yard.

Just then, Milo appeared on the sidewalk. He picked up the ball and brought it back. "You can't make them all, Jim," he told me.

"I can't even make ONE!" I said.

"Maybe you just need a little incentive," Milo suggested.

"A what?" I asked.

"You know, like how my dog, Tank, gets a treat for playing fetch," Milo explained. "You need a reward for making a shot."

"I'm not a dog, Milo," I told him.

"Maybe not," he said, "but you do look hungry."

I couldn't argue with that.

"Okay," I agreed. "But what's the reward?"

Milo reached into his vest pocket and pulled out a caramel-apple muffin. It was a little smooshed. But after one hundred and four laps and two hundred and four free throws, I'd have eaten the wrapper.

I grabbed for the muffin.

"Nuh-uh," said Milo, wagging his finger at me. "Here's the deal. You make a shot, you take a bite. You miss the shot, I take a bite."

"Deal," I said.

I stepped back with the ball and lined up for my first shot.

CLANK!

"One for me!" Milo exclaimed. He peeled back part of the wrapper and sunk his teeth into the ooey-gooey muffin. "Not bad." He licked his lips.

"Enjoy it," I told him, "because that's your last bite."

I picked up the ball and took another shot.

DONK!

"Grrrrr . . ." I growled, picking up the ball yet again.

CLANK!

DONK!

CLANK!

When I glanced over again, Milo was holding the last bite of the muffin. My arms and legs burned, sweat dripped into my eyes, and my stomach growled. I needed to make this shot.

I breathed deep, focused on the hoop, flicked the ball toward the basket, and . . .

DONK!

"NOOooOOOOooooOO!!" I cried.

"Better luck next time," said Milo, popping the last bite into his mouth.

"NEXT time?!" I screamed. "That was the last bite! And today, that was the last shot of the game! Just once, I'd like NEXT time to be THIS time!"

I grabbed the ball and threw up one last angry shot. **SWOOOOSH!**

"You did it, Jim! Way to go!" Milo exclaimed. "And now that you've done it once, I bet you'll never forget how. Just like riding a bike."

Maybe Milo was right. Maybe I'd finally found my rhythm. I just needed to repeat the same motion, and I'd be making shots every time.

"Put her there," said Milo, holding his hand up for a high-five.

I raised my arm and — "Ow!" I screamed out.

"Don't leave me hanging," Milo said, still waiting for his high-five.

"I've heard the saying 'practice makes perfect,'" I told him, "but it makes something else, too . . ."

"What's that?" Milo asked.

"Painful!" I replied, gritting my teeth.

"Nothing a little rest can't help," Milo said, waving goodbye. "See you at school tomorrow."

"See you," I said, unable to wave back.

CHAPTER FOUR

SORE SPORT

Turns out Milo was wrong . . .
again. When I woke up the next day,
I couldn't even lift my arms! They
felt like two heavy tuna fish barely
flopping at my sides.

I couldn't change my shirt, so I
wore the one I'd slept in. I couldn't lift
my spoon, so I sunk my face right into
the cereal bowl.

When I finally got to school, the day only got worse.

In math class, Mr. Donaldson wrote two problems on the board. "Any volunteers?" he asked the class.

Now I normally wasn't one to volunteer, but I finally (I mean, for the first time EVER!) knew the answer. There was only problem: I couldn't raise my hand.

I waited and waited and then finally — "I know! I know!" I shouted.

"Tsk! Tsk!" said Mr. Donaldson, itching his thick, bushy mustache. "I appreciate the enthusiasm, but what's the proper way to volunteer?"

On the other side of the classroom, Bobby Studwell raised his hand and quietly waited.

"Very good, Mr. Studwell," said Mr. Donaldson. "Please come to the front of the class."

Bobby looked at me and smirked.

"And, Mr. Nasium," Mr. Donaldson continued, "since you're so eager, why don't you go ahead and join him?"

Bobby was already writing his answer, so I hurried to the board.

I'm going to beat him at something, I thought, grabbing the dry-erase marker and reaching up to write.

"Ow!" I exclaimed.

"What's the matter, Nasium?" Bobby whispered. "Did you hurt your brain?" He laughed.

I couldn't let Bobby — or ANYONE — know that I was injured. If I did, I wouldn't even get the chance to play in this week's game. Coach Pittman would bench me for sure!

"HA! Very funny," I said, thinking fast. "But no, it's just painful watching you try to solve that problem."

"Shows what you know," said Bobby. "I'm already done."

When I looked up, Bobby had written "BUFFALOES #1" on the board.

The class all cheered for him.

"I'm afraid that's incorrect, Mr. Studwell," said Mr. Donaldson.

"Are you saying the Buffaloes aren't number one, sir?" asked Bobby.

"Booo!" the class all jeered.

"Ahem!" Mr. Donaldson quickly quieted the class. "Mr. Nasium, perhaps you'll take this assignment a bit more seriously."

I lifted my arm again, attempting to write the answer. "Ow!" I squealed quietly, pushing through the pain.

I pressed the marker against the board. My arm burned, a bead of sweat dripped from my forehead, and my hand began to shake.

I dropped my arm down to my side. It was no use. The only thing I'd managed to write was a couple small dots with a shaky, squiggly line underneath them.

"HAHAHAHA!" the class laughed.

At first I didn't know why my pain was so funny. Then I looked over at Mr. Donaldson. He crossed his arms over his chest and scowled at the board through his bushy mustache.

"A wise guy, huh?" Mr. Donaldson grunted.

I glanced up at the board. I realized my two dots and squiggly line looked more like two eyes and a bushy —

"Uh-oh," I gulped.

"Perhaps you two basketball stars need a time-out," said Mr. Donaldson, "in the principal's office!"

"You'll pay for this, Nasium," growled Bobby, following me out of the classroom.

I silently gulped again.

CHAPTER FIVE

DOGGONE INJURY

I wouldn't wish an afternoon in the principal's office on any kid (okay, maybe Bobby Studwell . . .), but on this particular day, the punishment ended up being more of a reward.

First, while in the principal's office, I didn't have to raise my arm once. (Although I did get a pain in my neck from all the head-nodding.)

Second, the principal's office was so busy, I ended up missing basketball practice. Don't get me wrong, I needed the practice. But at least I didn't have to explain to Coach Pittman why I couldn't raise my arms above my bellybutton.

By the way, turns out that the principal's office was so busy because of a little mistake on the lunch menu. Apparently, the menu read Stop Sign Pizza (pizza shaped like a, well, stop sign), but the cooks ended up serving Western Beans (a fancy name for franks 'n' beans). The students were not pleased with the change, to say the least.

Lastly, because I missed a practice, Coach Pittman thought it would be best if I sat out a few more. He wanted me to think about my "commitment to the team," as he put it. Funny, since my overcommitment had landed me in this spot to begin with.

Anyway, I was pretty much off scot-free. Except for one little detail — I still had to tell my parents. AND get them to sign a note from the principal. Okay, maybe that detail wasn't so little. In fact, it was kind of a big detail, which is why I decided to walk the long way home that afternoon.

At least I'd be able to enjoy an extra five minutes of freedom.

As I walked past the Bennett City park, I heard a voice call out, "Hey, Jim, heads up!"

I looked up and spotted a four-legged ball of fur, teeth, and drool barreling toward me. It was Milo's bulldog, Tank!

"Easy, boy!" I shouted. "Easy, boy!"

RUFF! RUFF!

Tank barked but didn't stop. I closed my eyes and braced myself, preparing to be slobberfied.

But nothing happened.

RUFF! RUFF! I heard again. I slowly opened my eyes.

Tank stood a foot in front of me with a fuzzy tennis ball at his feet. His tongue panted and his tail wagged.

Milo walked over. "He wants you to throw it," he told me.

"I'll try," I said.

I picked up the ball and a long string of glue-like slobber dripped off of it. I painfully pulled my arm back and threw the ball the best I could.

PLOP. PLOP. PLOP.

The ball landed less than five feet in front of me and slowly rolled to a stop. Before I could finish yelling "OW!," Tank was back, waiting for another throw.

"It's this doggone injury," I said.

"HAHA! Good one, Jim," said Milo.

"I'm serious, Milo," I told him. "I can't raise my hand above my head."

"Then why don't you try throwing underhand?" Milo suggested. "Like a softball pitcher."

It can't hurt, I thought, picking up the ball and giving it a toss.

To my surprise, it didn't hurt. At all. In fact, it felt pretty good.

"Wow! Nice throw, Jim," Milo said as Tank quickly returned with the ball. "Try that again. And this time, see if you can throw it all the way to that trash can over there." He pointed to a small wastebasket nearly a football field away.

I grabbed the ball from Tank, pulled back my arm, and then let loose an underhand throw.

FWOOOOOSH!

The tennis ball rocketed through the air like a comet, complete with a tail of slobber trailing behind it.

The throw had perfect backspin, perfect arc, perfect height . . . and this time, perfect distance.

CLANK! The ball landed right in the trash can.

"Nice shot!" Milo exclaimed. "Nothing but net — I mean, trash!"

"HA! If only I could shoot like that on the court," I said.

"Why can't you?" Milo wondered.

Before I could answer his question, I heard the thundering sound of footsteps — or rather, PAWsteps — heading toward me. Tank had tipped over the trash can and was bounding back in my direction with the ball.

"He's going to stop, right?" I nervously asked Milo.

Milo shrugged his shoulders.

WHAM-O!

Tank slammed into me like a, well, two-ton tank! He dropped the ball and started licking my face with his short, slobbery tongue.

"HAHAHA!" I laughed. "What does he want, Milo? What does he want?"

"Like I said, Tank always gets a treat for playing fetch," Milo said.

"HAHA! Then hurry . . . HAHA!" I said, trying to fend off the manic mutt. "Give him something! HAHA!"

Milo reached into his vest pocket and pulled out another caramel-apple muffin. He tossed the muffin in the air, and Tank leaped for it. **CHOMP!** He swallowed the tasty treat — wrapper and all — in one giant gulp!

"Where do you keep getting those muffins?" I asked, standing up.

"The bakery, of course," Milo joked. "Where else?"

I rolled my eyes and started walking away.

"Where are you going?" Milo asked.

"To take a shower," I said, wiping slobber from my mouth.

CHAPTER SIX

FOUL TROUBLE

The shower would have to wait. When I finally got home, my parents were waiting for me at the front door with their arms angrily crossed over their chests. Apparently, someone from the principal's office had called them.

I spent the next hour explaining everything.

After they heard the whole story, Mom and Dad decided not to punish me. They only had one condition: no more basketball until I could shoot the ball without any pain.

I headed upstairs, closed my bedroom door, and plopped down on the bed.

Without any more practice, I thought, *I'll never be ready for Saturday's big game.*

Just then, I remembered the question that Milo had asked me earlier. Why couldn't I shoot underhand on the basketball court anyway? As far as I knew, that wasn't against the rules.

And because shooting underhand didn't hurt, I wouldn't be breaking my parents' rule either.

"That's it!" I exclaimed.

I couldn't wait to give this new plan a shot.

CHAPTER SEVEN

GRANNY SHOT

BREEPBREEPBREEPBREEP!

My alarm sounded at 5:30 the next morning. I had set it for a half hour earlier than I normally wake up.

I quickly showered, washing off as much of the dried-on dog slobber that I could. Then I threw on clothes and shoes and dashed out to the garage.

I grabbed my basketball, dribbled onto the driveway, and lined up for a free throw. But instead of lifting the ball above my head, I held the ball down between my legs.

I focused on the hoop, breathed deep, and then I threw my arms up for an underhand shot.

SWOOSH!

The ball sailed right through the basket on my first try.

"Nothing but net!" I shouted.

"Jim, is that you?" I heard a voice call from above. I looked up and spotted my dad standing at the upstairs window.

"Have you already forgotten what we talked about last night?" he asked.

"No, Dad. I found a way to shoot without any pain," I explained. "Watch me."

I grabbed the ball, lowered it between my legs again, and shot another free throw.

SWOOSH!

"See?!" I proudly exclaimed.

"I guess I can't argue with that," said Dad. "Very impressive."

"Eh," I scoffed. "Probably just beginner's luck."

Dad smiled and closed the window.

I stepped back with the ball and lined up for another shot.

SWOOSH!

I picked up the ball again and took another shot.

SWOOSH!

And another . . .

SWOOSH!

And another . . .

SWOOSH!

"Six for six!" I shouted, jumping up and down with excitement. "Time for lucky number seven!"

I took the shot. **SWOOSH!**

"HAHAHA!" I heard a familiar, wicked laugh from nearby.

At the end of my driveway, I spotted Bobby Studwell and Tommy Strong sitting atop their bikes. They were on their way to school.

"Nice granny shot, Nasium," Bobby joked, laughing.

"HAHAHA! Granny shot! Good one, Bobby," echoed Tommy Strong.

"Huh?" I asked, puzzled. "What are you talking about?"

"A granny shot," Bobby repeated. "That's the way my grandmother would shoot a basketball."

"HAHAHAHAHA!" they both laughed again. Then they started biking away.

"I hope you aren't planning to shoot like that in Saturday's game," Bobby called out as he disappeared down the sidewalk.

Not anymore, I thought.

CHAPTER EIGHT

TIP-OFF

BZZZZZZZZZZZRRRRRRT!

A buzzer sounded in the Bennett City Elementary gymnasium. It was Saturday and before I knew it, the big game was underway.

Our opponents, the Jackrabbits, were living up to their team's name. They were off to a fast start.

By the end of the first quarter, the Jackrabbits had taken a 12–2 lead.

I couldn't take much responsibility for our team being behind. I hadn't helped them try to catch up either. In fact, I hadn't played a single minute.

However, I was succeeding at one thing: bench-warming. I guessed sometimes practice really did make perfect . . .

BREEEEEP!

Just then, I heard Coach Pittman blow his whistle. "Time-out!" he shouted at the referee.

The starting five players hurried off the court and plopped onto the bench.

Coach Pittman paced back and forth in front of us, grumbling. Then I heard him say some familiar words: "I'm going to mix things up a bit."

I felt a nervous pit in my stomach, and then I heard the three words that I had feared.

"Nasium, you're in!" Coach Pittman instructed.

"Go get 'em, Jim!" said Milo, giving me a slap on the back.

I slowly shuffled onto the court, and the game quickly started back up. For nearly the entire second quarter, I ran up and down the court as our team slowly chipped away at the lead.

With twenty seconds left in the first half, we only trailed by two points. The scoreboard read, "BUFFALOES 20, JACKRABBITS 22."

I hadn't touched the ball once, but at least I was on the court. I felt like a part of the team.

It's not that I was afraid of shooting the ball. During the past week, I'd taken 357 granny shots, and I had made 356 of them. I only missed one because Milo's dog had mistaken me for the mail carrier and tackled me mid-shot. Otherwise, I would've been shooting one hundred percent. One hundred percent of *granny* shots, that is.

And that was the problem!

I had two choices:

1.) Shoot like everyone else and possibly miss a painful shot, or . . .

2.) Take a funny-looking shot and have a 99.9999 percent chance of making it.

Fortunately, it looked like I'd have until at least the second half to make that decision —

"Jim, heads up!" I suddenly heard someone shout.

I looked up and a pass was headed right for me. I caught the ball and was quickly surrounded by defenders.

I had to make a decision: option #1 or option #2.

Think. Think, I told myself, unable to decide.

Then . . .

BZZZZZZZZZZRRRRRRT!

The buzzer sounded, and the first half was over.

"Nice going, Nasium," growled Bobby Studwell.

I'll be going, all right, I thought. *Going home.*

CHAPTER NINE

HALFTIME NO-SHOW

As the team headed to the locker room for halftime, I headed out the front door of the school. I wasn't going to be a hoop hero. I'd always be a basket case.

BARK! BARK! BARK!

I heard a familiar bark and spotted Milo's dog near the school's bike rack.

Tank waited patiently for Milo to return. But when he spotted me, he came bounding over with a tennis ball in his slobbery jaws.

BARK! BARK! BARK!

"Not today, boy," I told him. "I'm not in the mood to play fetch."

I started walking toward home. Tank followed closely behind.

BARK! BARK! BARK!

"No, Tank!" I shouted. "Go back and wait for Milo!"

Tank jumped at the back of my legs. **BARK! BARK! BARK!** He dropped the ball at my feet.

"Fine!" I finally said.

I picked up the tennis ball. Without thinking, I tossed the ball as hard as I could. Overhand!

The ball sailed all the way across the school parking lot. By the time Tank returned with it, he was already exhausted.

I raised both arms into the air. They felt great! I guessed I had rested them long enough.

Maybe I can shoot like everyone else, I thought to myself. *Or at least I can try.*

I ran back inside to the locker room.

CHAPTER TEN

UNDERACHIEVER

The second half went by much like the first: right in front of my eyes! I spent all of it on the bench.

But even without me in the game (or maybe because of me out of the game), we narrowed the Jackrabbits' lead. Our team was down by three points with eight seconds remaining.

The scoreboard read, "BUFFALOES 31, JACKRABBITS 34."

BREEEEEEEEEEEEP! The referee blew his whistle. Tommy Strong had fouled out of the game.

"It's not fair!!" Tommy whined, plopping down on the bench.

Coach Pittman pointed at me, and this time I hustled onto the court.

"Jim!" I heard Milo call.

I looked back at the bench. Milo held a caramel-apple muffin in his hand. He gave the ooey-gooey treat a long sniff and then gave me a wink.

I knew what I had to do.

This time, I desperately tried to escape my defender and get open for the inbound pass. I zigged and zagged, squeaking back and forth across the court.

Finally, the ball came to me. I caught the pass and headed up the court as fast as I could.

8 seconds . . .

7 seconds . . .

6 seconds . . .

Right at the three-point line, I stopped and pulled up for a shot. But then I thought better. Option #2. I lowered the ball between my legs and let loose the ultimate granny shot!

Perfect backspin, perfect arc, perfect height, perfect distance, and . . .

SWOOSH!

Milo, Brad Barker, Ricky Howard, Justin Springfield, Dudley Schumaker, and all the benchwarmers, sixth men, or sixteenth men stormed the court.

Milo held up his hand. "High-five!" he said.

"How about a LOW-five?" I suggested instead.

I was a hoops hero, after all . . . for about two seconds. The referee blew the whistle. My foot had been over the three-point line. The shot only counted as two points. We had lost by one!

"Oh, well," said Milo, "it was still a great shot, Jim."

"HAHA! Yeah, a *granny* shot!" Bobby laughed.

"What's so funny about grannies?" I heard a voice say from behind.

It was Coach Pittman's grandma!

"Um, uh, nothing," Bobby stuttered.

Milo and I laughed.

"Now about your reward." Milo opened his hand to reveal a half-eaten, sweat-covered muffin. "It was a long eight seconds," he said.

"That's okay, Milo," I said. "Making that shot was sweet enough."

AUTHOR

Marty McKnight is a freelance writer from St. Paul, Minnesota. He has written many chapter books for young readers.

ILLUSTRATOR

Chris Jones is a children's illustrator based in Canada. He has worked as both a graphic designer and an illustrator. His illustrations have appeared in several magazines and educational publications, and he also has numerous graphic novels and children's books to his credit. Chris is inspired by good music, books, long walks, and generous amounts of coffee.

BASKETBALL JOKES!

Q: Why was Cinderella so bad at basketball practice?

A: She kept running away from the coach!

Q: Did you hear about the baby who crawled out onto the basketball court?

A: She was penalized for dribbling!

Q: Why can't basketball players ever take vacations?

A: They're not allowed to travel!

Q: How did the basketball players make such a mess at the bakery?

A: They kept dunkin' donuts!

Q: Why are there so many lawyers at a basketball game?

A: They stick around in case anyone has to go to court!

Q: Why do fish make terrible basketball players?

A: They keep getting caught in the net!

Q: What is a personal foul?

A: Your very own chicken!

JIM NASIUM IS A Football Fumbler
BY MARTY McKNIGHT & CHRIS JONES

JIM NASIUM IS A Basket Case
BY MARTY McKNIGHT & CHRIS JONES

JIM NASIUM IS A Soccer Goofball
BY MARTY McKNIGHT & CHRIS JONES

JIM NASIUM IS A Hockey Hazard
BY MARTY McKNIGHT & CHRIS JONES